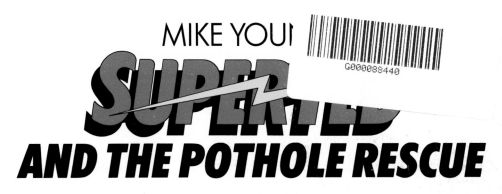

MIKE YOUNG

SUPERTED
AND THE POTHOLE RESCUE

Illustrations by
Rob Lee and David Blake

Muller, Blond & White

Spottyman was running a vacuum cleaner up the walls of SuperTed's space station. Suddenly the alarm went off. A girl's face appeared on the video screen.

"Help! Please help!"

Spotty was making so much noise that SuperTed could not hear a thing. "Will you turn that off, Spotty," he shouted.

"Keep your fur on, SuperTed," said Spotty, grumpily, but he turned the machine off all the same. SuperTed turned to hear the girl's message.

"My friend is trapped in an underground tunnel," explained the girl, tearfully. "The water's rising. If we don't get her out soon, she'll drown."

SuperTed did not wait to hear more. He said his magic word and, after Spotty had put on his rocket pack, the two friends shot towards the earth.

They flew down over the mountains and soon landed near the girl.

"Thank goodness you're here," she said, hurriedly, and she handed them each a helmet. "Quick! Put these on. Potholing is very dangerous. You've got to be properly equipped." Then she turned to Spotty. "You won't need that rocket pack," she added. "It won't be much use to you underground."

Spotty began to complain. "I can't wear this helmet," he said. He tossed it away with a shrug. "It's got stripes."

The girl did not stop to listen. She led them over a ridge and, before they knew it, they were all sliding down a muddy hole in the ground.

They were in a sort of mud slide, which led deep beneath the earth. Recent rain had made the surface very slippery and all three of them hurtled downwards at tremendous speed.

SuperTed shuddered as he saw the sides of the rocky tunnel flash past on either side, lit by the shaky light of his helmet. Then he hit a bump and his helmet went spinning into the darkness.

It was all very frightening, but soon he and the girl emerged into a huge underground cavern. Beneath them, a fast-flowing river ran across the cave and out through a tunnel. Bobbing up and down on it was the girl's dinghy. SuperTed turned and looked back up the tunnel. "Where's Spotty?"

Spotty was having trouble. He kept on banging his head against the roof of the tunnel and then he totally lost control, spinning downwards together with an avalanche of small stones. He shot out of the end of the tunnel, straight into SuperTed and the girl.

"Aaagh!" They all fell towards the river. SuperTed and the girl landed in the dinghy, but the force of their fall made the boat bounce away from the rock, and Spotty fell into the water with a splash.

The girl began to paddle. "Hurry," she said. "We've got no time to lose. We must rescue my friend!"

The dinghy began to move off, leaving Spotty swimming behind. SuperTed leant over the back of the boat and tried to help him. "I wish you'd hurry up, Spotty!"

"I'm coming!" called Spotty and soon SuperTed was helping him into the dinghy.

The current became stronger and stronger as the river narrowed towards a crack in the rock. Water frothed around the sides of the dinghy, splashing the girl in the face.

"Pulsating Prunes! We're going too fast!" cried SuperTed.

"It's the current!" the girl shouted back at him. "Watch your head as we go through here!"

She flattened herself on the floor of the boat and SuperTed ducked as low as he could, but Spotty was too upset to do anything.

"I'm not going to listen until I'm treated with a little more respect," he said angrily. At that moment the dinghy disappeared into a low tunnel and Spotty banged his head against the rock with a resounding crack.

In the tunnel, all was dark. Above the noise of splashing water they could hear a deep droning sound.

"What's that rumbling noise?" asked SuperTed.

"It sounds more like a buzzing in the ears to me," said Spotty, who was still a little dazed.

The noise became louder and louder. When they rounded a corner in the tunnel, they saw what it was. They were heading over a huge waterfall!

"Quick! Jump!" shouted the girl. She grabbed SuperTed and hauled him onto a ledge. Spotty was too slow. Frozen with horror, he clung to the dinghy as it tumbled over the edge.

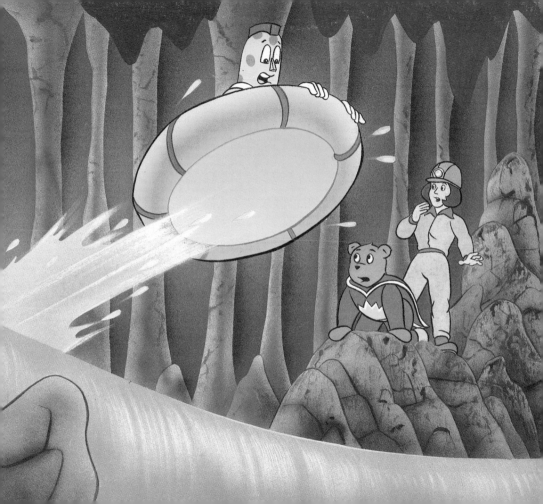

SuperTed fired his rocket boots at full power. "Hang on, Spotty!" he called and he flew down into the cascading water.

The force of the waterfall knocked him sideways, but he caught the edge of the dinghy and, flying underneath it, pushed it away from the wall of water.

He hauled the rubber boat on to a ledge of rock and then, suddenly, groaned with despair. Spotty was no longer in it.

"Spotty! Spotty! Where are you?" he shouted at the top of his voice.

From somewhere in the distance they heard a faint reply. "Help! Help!" came a feeble cry, but it was not Spotty's voice.

"I think it's my friend," cried the girl.

The girl dashed through a crack in the rock into another passage. Sure enough, there was her friend. Her foot was trapped under a huge slab and the water had risen right up to her neck. If someone did not free her soon, she would drown.

The girl tried desperately to haul the rock away, but it was too heavy. "It's no use, Linda. I can't shift it. Where's SuperTed? We need his help. SuperTed!"

SuperTed was still looking for Spotty. He dived in and out of the waterfall, but could find no sign of his friend.

By now, the girl was beginning to panic. Linda's head was underwater. "SuperTed! Quick! She's going to drown."

With an unhappy sigh, SuperTed flew down the passage towards them. As he did so, rocks began to fall around him. The tunnel was collapsing!

SuperTed dived under the water and pulled the slab of rock away from Linda's legs. She rose to the surface and took a huge breath of air. "Oh, thank you, SuperTed," she sighed.

After the fall of rock, a crack had opened in the roof above them. "That's daylight up there," called the girl. Carefully she began to help her friend back to the open air.

SuperTed looked along the passage. The way back to the waterfall was blocked by a huge wall of boulders. He would never be able to get back to Spotty.

"Oh, Spotty," he sobbed. "I'll never see you again . . . and I didn't even have time to say goodbye." As he stood there, despairing and upset, he felt the water swirl around his legs. "The water! It's coming from the ground somewhere. There must be an underground passage!"

Then he dived under the water once more.

He pushed aside boulder after boulder, speeding through shafts and tunnels flooded with water until he emerged eventually at the foot of the waterfall.

"Spotty!" he shouted in desperation. "Where are you?"

Spotty had banged his head when he went over the edge, and he had fallen, unconscious, on to a shelf of rock hidden behind the waterfall. When he heard SuperTed calling, he stood up and, still very dazed, looked out over the ledge. The force of the waterfall hit him in the back of the neck and sent him tumbling over the edge once more.

Beneath him, SuperTed gasped with surprise. There was his friend, falling straight towards him. He flew forwards and caught Spotty in his arms with a flourish.

"Got you!" he yelled with delight. "Oh Spotty, I've never known anyone take so long to fall down a waterfall!"

Later, SuperTed and Spotty helped the girls to the surface, where a helicopter was waiting to take them to hospital.

"Come on, Spotty," he said. "Help me lift Linda."

"Oh, all right," said Spotty, but as he leant forward, he banged his head against the doorway of the helicopter.

"Spotty! Spotty!" called SuperTed, but there was no reply.

Once again, Spotty was out cold.

Books in the SuperTed series